Giraffe was sad. Giraffe said he was still hungry. But Wolf wasn't bothered.

At playtime, Wolf never thought about others either. He liked playing on the swing. But he never thought about anyone else **wanting a turn**. He said he wanted to stay on the swing forever!

The others were cross. They said he was **unkind**
for only thinking about himself.

Worse still, Wolf wouldn't **share** his toys.
When Monkey came to play, he never let him play
with his two green tractors.

Monkey loved playing with tractors. But Wolf said they were **his**, and no one else could play with them. He didn't think about Monkey's feelings. It made Monkey very sad.

One day, Mr Croc said everyone could play cricket after school. Wolf got the cricket bat first. He hit the ball a long way. Koala tried to catch it, but she fell over.

Koala was **upset**. Everyone stopped playing to help her ... everyone **except wolf**.

Wolf wanted to keep playing. He **didn't think** about Koala. He didn't think how Koala was feeling. Everyone was cross with Wolf. They said they didn't want to play with him anymore.

Wolf was **upset**. He didn't like everyone being cross with him. Mr Croc talked to him. He asked Wolf how he would feel if no one helped or shared with him ... or thought about his feelings.

14

Wolf said he wouldn't like it at all! Mr Croc said it was important to think about how others were feeling. He said it was much **nicer to be kind**.

Then Mr Croc asked Wolf what he could do to **put things right**. Wolf had a think.

He said he should **say sorry** to Koala. He said
he should think about others' feelings. He said he
should be **kind and helpful**, too. Mr Croc said
they were good ideas.

The next day, Wolf **tried hard** to think of others. He helped Mum fold up the washing. Mum said he was **very kind**.

He **helped his little sister** put on her bag.
She gave him a hug.

Later, Mum had a phone call from Monkey's mum. Monkey was ill in bed. He was feeling very **sad and lonely**. He was missing all his friends.

Mum said she would bake him some little cakes to **cheer him up**. Wolf helped her.

Then Wolf had a big think. He **felt very sorry** for Monkey. He thought about **how he would feel** if he were ill in bed.

He didn't like it at all. He wanted to make Monkey feel happy again. Then he had a **good idea**.

Wolf went up to his bedroom. He got out his two green tractors. He wrote a big label on one tractor. It said: "To Monkey from Wolf".

Wolf and Mum went to Monkey's house.
Mum gave him the cakes. Wolf gave Monkey
the green tractor. Monkey was very pleased.

Wolf and Monkey played with the tractors all afternoon. Monkey said Wolf was very kind. Wolf said it was much nicer to be kind and to think of others' feelings. He said it made everyone feel happy.

A note about sharing this book

The *Behaviour Matters* series has been developed to provide a starting point for further discussion on children's behaviour both in relation to themselves and others. The series is set in the jungle with animal characters reflecting typical behaviour traits often seen in young children.

Wolf Thinks of Others
This story encourages the reader to develop empathy for others by examining situations familiar to young children.

How to use the book
The book is designed for adults to share with either an individual child, or a group of children, and as a starting point for discussion.

The book also provides visual support and repeated words and phrases to build reading confidence.

Before reading the story
Choose a time to read when you and the children are relaxed and have time to share the story.

Spend time looking at the illustrations and talk about what the book might be about before reading it together.

Encourage children to employ a phonics first approach to tackling new words by sounding the words out.

After reading, talk about the book with the children.

- Spend time discussing what the book is about.

- Ask the children to recall situations where someone hadn't thought about their feelings; examples might be not sharing toys fairly or not being allowed a turn on something. How did they feel? Encourage the children to share their experiences with the others and to wait patiently for their turn to speak.

- Now ask the children to recall situations where someone had thought about their feelings. What happened? How did they feel?

- Ask the children why they think it is important to consider other people's feelings.

- Invite the children to help you make a poster for the classroom about thinking of others. Possible suggestions could be:
  Our class likes to think of others because:
  ... we are kind ... we are helpful ... we are friendly.

  Encourage the children to think of as many positive aspects of this topic as possible. Then invite the children to draw pictures on the poster to illustrate examples of how they think of others and to write a caption by each drawing.

For Isabelle, William A, William G, George, Max, Emily,
Leo, Caspar, Felix, Tabitha, Phoebe and Harry –S.G.

Franklin Watts
First published in 2022 by
The Watts Publishing Group

Editor: Jackie Hamley
Designer: Cathryn Gilbert and Peter Scoulding

A CIP catalogue record for this book is available
from the British Library.

ISBN 978 1 4451 7996 4 (hardback)
ISBN 978 1 4451 7997 1 (paperback)
ISBN 978 1 4451 8374 9 (ebook)

Printed in China

Franklin Watts
An imprint of
Hachette Children's Group
Part of The Watts Publishing Group
Carmelite House
50 Victoria Embankment
London EC4Y 0DZ

An Hachette UK company.
www.hachette.co.uk

www.hachettechildrens.co.uk

MIX
Paper from
responsible sources
FSC
www.fsc.org
FSC® C104740